D1595045

What's Growing in Grandma's Garden

What's Growing in Grandma's Garden

written by

Susan Soares

A Book to Help Grownups Have a
Conversation With Children About Cannabis

My Grandmother loves plants. She has lots of them. When I come over to her house we like to work together in her garden. She says that she has two green thumbs. They look normal to me!

Most of the plants are for eating or for medicine. She has lots of vegetables, fruit and different herbs for medicine.

Sometimes we pick
something in her garden
and eat it right away.
My favorite is carrots.

They taste so much better when you eat them from Grandma's garden. She says it's because they are so fresh. Fresh is BEST!

Roly poly bugs eat our strawberries and tomatoes. When I come over, we go roly poly hunting. They turn into a round ball when they see people. I'm going to get you Mr. Roly Poly!!

Lady bugs eat some of the bad bugs. I love the praying mantis. They have Ninja skills.

Grandma has some plants
that are extra special
to her. She keeps them
locked in her greenhouse.
She says it's called
cannabis. She uses it to
make medicine and relax.

She says that I can look,
but not touch.

It's time for lunch. Grandma is getting some of her medicine and I'm looking for something I can eat from the garden.

Picking sweet potatoes is fun.
You never know how many you
are going to find!

Grandma cuts the pretty green cannabis leaves and blends them into a fruit smoothie. That's her favorite lunch. We are going to make sweet potato fries for me!

The cannabis leaves are so pretty.
I want to have some. Grandma
says they are just for grownups.

I asked Grandma why some things are just for grownups. She drew a brain for me. I colored in some of the parts. She showed me what all the different parts of the brain do.

She said that my brain is still growing
just like the plants in the garden
and I need to feed it only things that
will help it grow. I want my brain
to be as strong and fast as it can
be just like a super computer!

Grandma's knee hurts after so much sidewalk chalk art. She puts her medicine on her knee while I play with her train set.

My knees don't hurt. I guess there are some good things about not being a grown up!

On Sundays, we have a bar b q with our family and friends. Grandma cooks such good food!

The grownups do grownup things and the kids play hide and seek. There are some good places to hide in Grandma's garden. One is so good, no one has ever found me there!

Grandma always packs up the leftovers for us and fresh veggies from the garden so we can have them at home.

I love Grandma and her garden. When I grow up, I'm going to have a garden too!

Susan Soares
7139 E. Coralite Street
Long Beach, California 90808

Ordering Information:
Quantity sales. Special discounts are available on quantity purchases
by corporations, associations, and others. For details, contact
the author at the address above or call 336.420.6149.

ISBN 978-0-359-67572-2

United States Copyright Office Registration Number TXu 2-135-831

Special Thanks to Jeff "Woody" Fife from The Woody Show for inspiring the writing of this book and all of my beautiful and brilliant grandchildren that deserve to "just say know".